# Making God Happy: A Baseball Story

# Making God Happy: A Baseball Story

**A.J. Chilson**

# Making God Happy: A Baseball Story



This book is a work of fiction. Named locations are used fictitiously, and characters and incidents are the product of the author's imagination. Any resemblance to actual events or places or persons, living or dead, is entirely coincidental.



Published by
Lighthouse Christian Publishing
SAN 257-4330
5531 Dufferin Drive
Savage, Minnesota, 55378
United States of America

www.lighthousechristianpublishing.com

## *DEDICATION*

*First of all, I'd like to dedicate this book to my father. My Dad never got to play in the major leagues, but he's an All-Star in the game of life.*

*Second, I'd like to give a shout-out to my pastor and fellow book writer, Todd Boddy. He, too, is an All-Star at what he does.*

*To all my friends and loved ones, thank you for being there for me when I needed an All-Star for encouragement.*

*Last but not least, I'd like to give all the glory and praise to The Ultimate All-Star, Jesus Christ. He's been there for me when the going got tough. He'll be there for you, as well. Trust in Jesus, and everything will be all right.*

"So, whether you eat or drink, or whatever you do, do all to the glory of God."

1 Corinthians 10:31 ESV

T
7

**I love to play baseball. It's my favorite game of all.**

**I like to play with my teammates. They're my friends.**

**Sometimes, we play until the day ends.**

**My favorite position is shortstop. There, I field the ball on a hop.**

8

**Then I toss it to the second baseman Clay…**

3

**who throws the ball to the first baseman Jim.**

**Double play!**

**When I take my turn at the plate, I wait for the right pitch to hit. And I wait, and wait.**

7

**Then I swing the bat. Thwack! I hit a long one.**

12

**It's going... it's going... it's gone. Home run!**

**My teammates are happy for me.**

T

**But most importantly, I make God happy. For when I play baseball, I give Him my very best. Because if it weren't for God, no one would be blessed.**

# POEM VERSION

**I love to play baseball.**

**It's my favorite game of all.**

**I like to play with my teammates. They're my friends.**

**Sometimes, we play until the day ends.**

**My favorite position is shortstop.**

**There, I field the ball on a hop.**

**Then I toss it to the second baseman Clay,**

**who throws the ball to the first baseman Jim. Double play!**

**When I take my turn at the plate,**

**I wait for the right pitch to hit. And I wait, and wait.**

**Then I swing the bat. Thwack! I hit a long one.**

**It's going... it's going... it's gone. Home run!**

**My teammates are happy for me.**

**But most importantly, I make God happy.**

**For when I play baseball, I give Him my very best.**

**Because if it weren't for God, no one would be blessed.**

**END**